P9-DYJ-430

INDIAN TWO FEET AND HIS EAGLE FEATHER

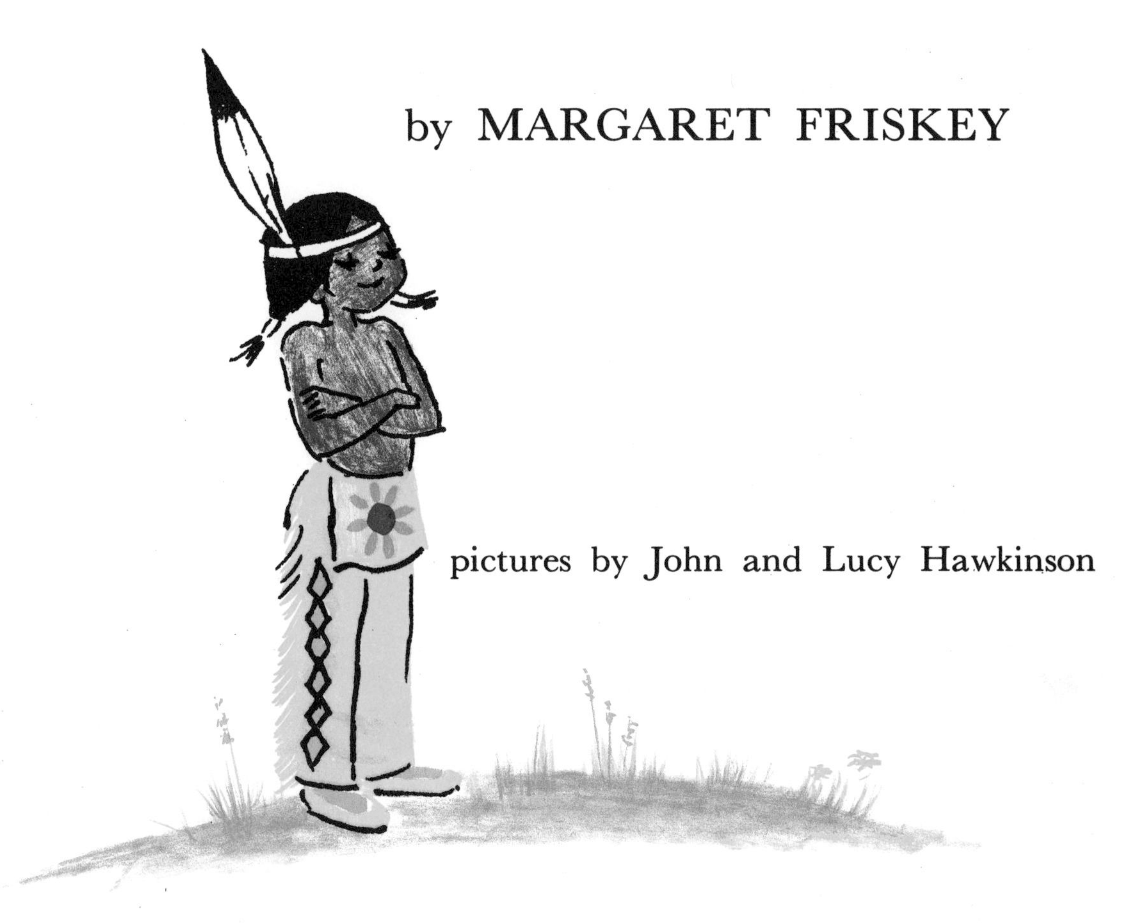

by MARGARET FRISKEY

pictures by John and Lucy Hawkinson

CHILDRENS PRESS, CHICAGO

Published simultaneously in Canada

Library of Congress Catalog Card Number: 67-20101

6 7 8 9 10 11 12 13 14 15 16 17 18 19 20 21 22 23 24 25 R 75 74 73 72

There was a little Indian

with a feather in his hair.

He had a little horse,

and he could ride,

ride,

ride.

One day when the sun
was bright,
and the sky
was blue,
he rode.
He was wise in the ways
of his Indian brothers.
He knew the cave
where the black bear lived.

He knew where the eagle
had her nest.

And where the red fox
hid her kits.

He knew where the beavers
had a dam,
and where the fish darted
through the deep pool above it.

Indian Two Feet galloped

along the stream.

Faster and faster went his horse.

The sound of the pound

of his horse's feet

made his heart sing.

"I'm an IN-di-an, IN-di-an, IN-di-an,

IN-di-an! Proud-of-it, proud-of-it,

proud-of-it, too. Brave as a buffalo,

buffalo, buffalo. Brave as a buffalo,

buffalo bull!"

The shadow of an eagle

crossed his path.

Surely a sign that he stood tall

among his people.

Swift as an eagle! An eagle! An eagle!

Indian Two Feet galloped

into his village.

The circle of warriors looked at him.
Their looks were long and dark.

"So!" said one. "Our little sparrow
thinks he is a hawk."

"He grows," said another. "He is tall
as a reed beside the stream."

Indian Two Feet's heart sank.

He thought, "Does it not please them
that I grow tall?"

But he stood silent before the men,
the wise ones.

"My son," said his father, "soon you
will be a man. In our tribe,
he who has the feather
of an eagle must earn it."
Indian Two Feet took the feather
from his hair. He laid it before his
father. His father had spoken.

Indian Two Feet felt like a child again
without his feather.

"Come," he said to his horse. "I will
show that I am brave. I will walk
into the cave of the bear."

Two small cubs played before the cave.

They rolled on the ground with each other.

Indian Two Feet walked toward the cave.

Suddenly the mother bear growled at him.

She stood up on her hind feet.

She was big. She was ENORMOUS!

Indian Two Feet jumped on his horse
and galloped away.

"You're a coward, a coward, a coward,
a coward!" the hoofs seemed to say.

That night Indian Two Feet

said to his father,

"I wanted to be brave. But

I was not. I ran from the

angry mother bear."

"It is a foolish Indian who angers

a mother bear," said his father.

The next day, Indian Two Feet
said to his horse, “Come, I will
show that I am brave. I will climb
the pine to the eagle’s nest.”
Away he galloped.

Two baby eagles opened their mouths
when they heard him coming.
Suddenly the mother eagle
swept down on the nest.
Her talons were sharp.
Her eyes gleamed.
Indian Two Feet slid down the tree,
and onto his horse.

"I wanted to be brave," he told his father.

"I climbed to the eagle's nest. I saw the young birds. But the mother eagle frightened me away."

"It is a stupid Indian who makes an eagle angry," said his father.

One day thunder rolled

across the sky.

A hunter rode into the village.

"Buffalo!" he cried.

"How many?"

"They spring up like grass

on the prairie."

"Where?"

"Half a day's ride beyond

the mountain."

The warriors made ready for the hunt.
Indian Two Feet wanted to go, too.
"Stay with the women," said his father.
"Catch some fish for them in the
deep pool."
Indian Two Feet started to say,
"I'm brave as a buffalo," but
the words died in his throat.

Indian Two Feet rode slowly
along the stream, under the
dark, unfriendly sky.
"I will go to the den of the fox,"
he said. "I will not anger the
mother fox. I will say to her,
'Give me one of your kits. I
will feed it and care for it.' "

The den of the fox was empty.
The mother fox had taken her kits
to higher ground.
Lightning flashed. Thunder rolled.
Great drops of rain fell. Split! Splat!
And then it poured.

Indian Two Feet turned his horse
toward the pool above the beaver dam.
He had been told to catch some fish.

The wind blew.

Waves rose on the pond.

A tree crashed into the water.

It swept down against the beaver dam.

It made a small hole in the dam.

Water rushed through the hole
in the dam.
The hole grew bigger.

Indian Two Feet forgot about the fish.

He thought of the village.

The village would be under water

when the dam broke.

Away he galloped toward the village.

By the time the flood came,

the village was safe on

higher ground.

The next day the hunters returned.

They were happy about the hunt.

There was meat for food. There was
fur for warm robes. There would be skin
for new tepees, and bones for needles.

But most of all, the men were happy
to see that the village was safe.

Indian Two Feet said to his father,

"I wanted to be brave. But the fox had moved her kits to higher ground. I wanted to catch a fish. But the dam was breaking. I rode to the village to help them move."

Indian Two Feet's father found the
eagle feather. He put it in
the boy's hair. "You have earned
your feather. You were as wise
as the fox who moved her kits.
Being wise is the first part
of being brave. Someday you
will be a great hunter."

Indian Two Feet galloped away.

His horse's hoofs pounded to the
beat of his heart.

"I'm an IN-di-an, IN-di-an, IN-di-an,
IN-di-an. Proud-of-it. Proud-of-it.
Proud-of-it, too."

His eagle feather bounced up and down.

He waved at the bear.

And he waved at the eagle.

He waved at the fox on top of the hill.

He stopped and watched the wise beavers.
They were brave enough to mend the dam
that was their home.

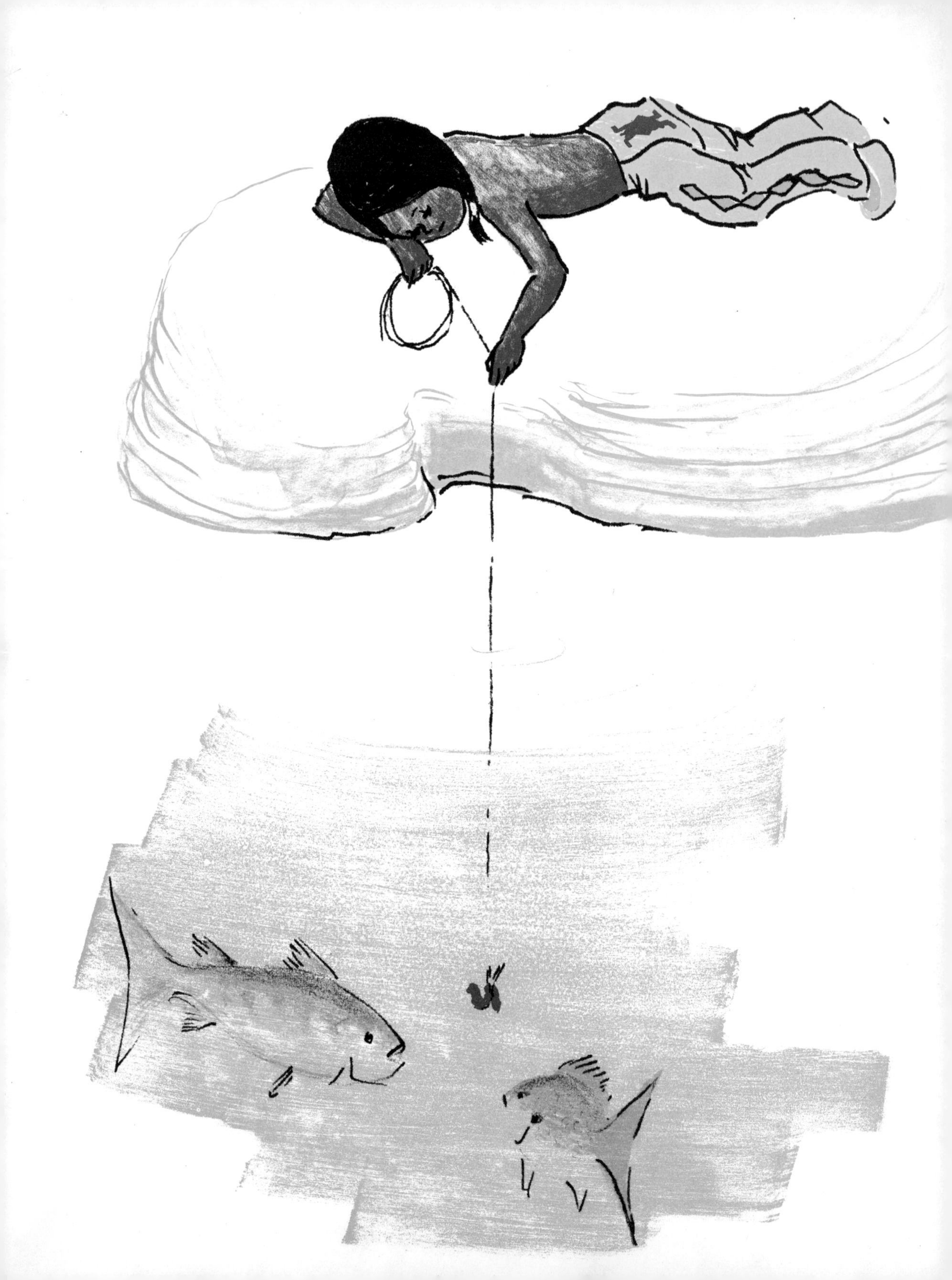